BELUGA PASSAGE

SMITHSONIAN OCEANIC COLLECTION

For my husband, Allan Haight,
and my fifth grade teacher, Florine Klatt
— L.L.

To Kris, Frank D., and Miriam,
all of whom are lifetime members of my pod.
Thank you for your love and support.
— J.D.W.

Book Design: Shields & Partners, Westport, CT

First Edition 1996
10 9 8 7 6 5 4 3 2 1
Printed in Singapore

Acknowledgements:
   Our very special thanks to Dr. Charles Handley of the Department of Vertebrate Zoology at the Smithsonian's
National Museum of Natural History for his curatorial review.
   The illustrator would also like to give his special thanks to Fran Hackett and Rick Miller of New York's Aquarium
for Wildlife Conservation, as well as to ace beluga photographer, David Roels, and the Vancouver Aquarium.

Library of Congress Cataloging-in-Publication Data

Lingemann, Linda, 1951-

Beluga passage / written by Linda Lingemann ; illustrated by Jon Weiman.
        p.   cm.
Summary: Beluga, her mother, and their pod of white whales face many dangers while migrating from the freezing
Arctic Ocean to the warmer waters of the Bering Sea.
        ISBN 1-56899-314-5
1. White whale — Juvenile fiction. [1. White whale — Fiction. 2. Whales — Fiction.]
I. Weiman, Jon 1956 - ill. II. Title.
        PZ10.3.L6455Be   1996   96-12642
        [E]— dc20   CIP
                                                                 AC

BELUGA PASSAGE

by **Linda Lingemann**   *Illustrated by* **Jon Weiman**

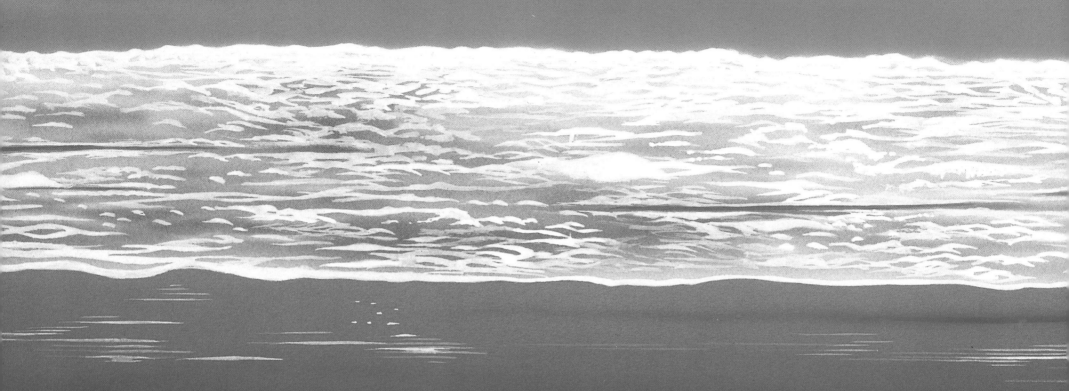

In the frigid Arctic Ocean, Beluga Calf and her mother glide
to the surface and breathe deeply through their blowholes.
The water churns and rolls around them, for they are not
alone. It is fall and thousands of "white whales" are on the move.
They are escaping a cold and deadly enemy — *ice*. Spreading from
the north, the ice is forming a solid crust on the ocean. The belugas
must stay ahead of the crust, or they will be trapped beneath it.
Racing the ice pack, they travel south toward the Bering Sea.

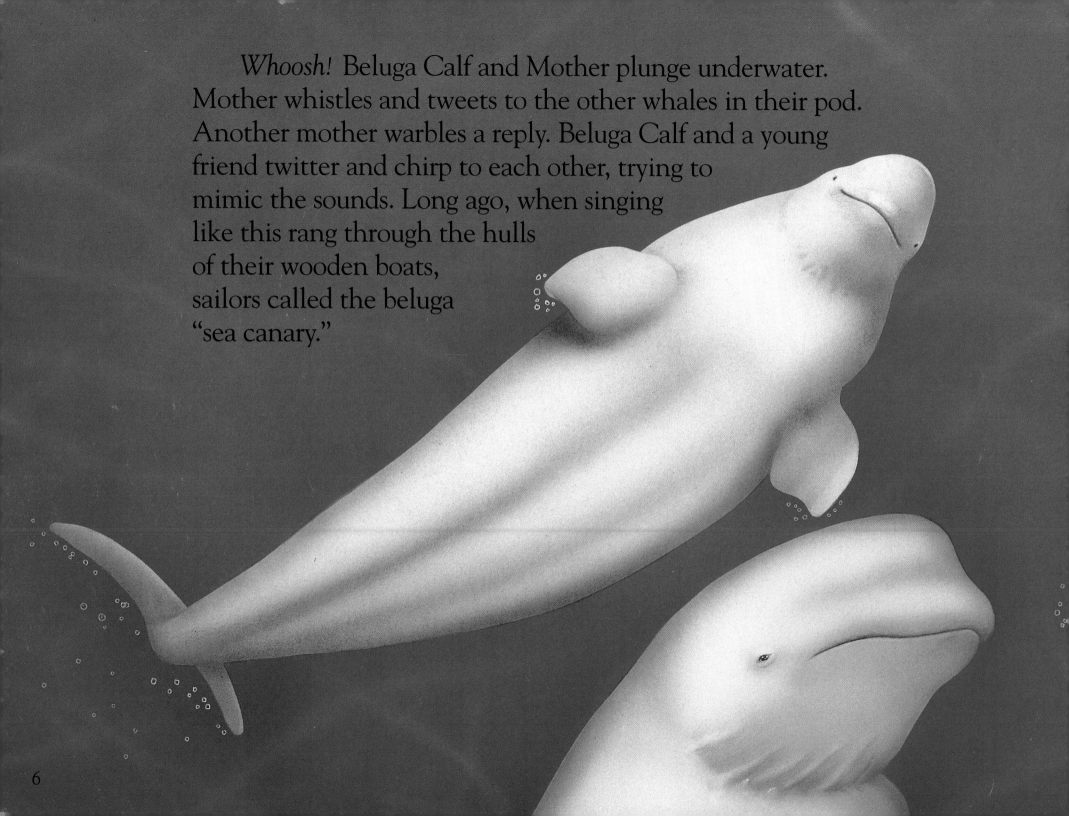

Whoosh! Beluga Calf and Mother plunge underwater.
Mother whistles and tweets to the other whales in their pod.
Another mother warbles a reply. Beluga Calf and a young
friend twitter and chirp to each other, trying to
mimic the sounds. Long ago, when singing
like this rang through the hulls
of their wooden boats,
sailors called the beluga
"sea canary."

6

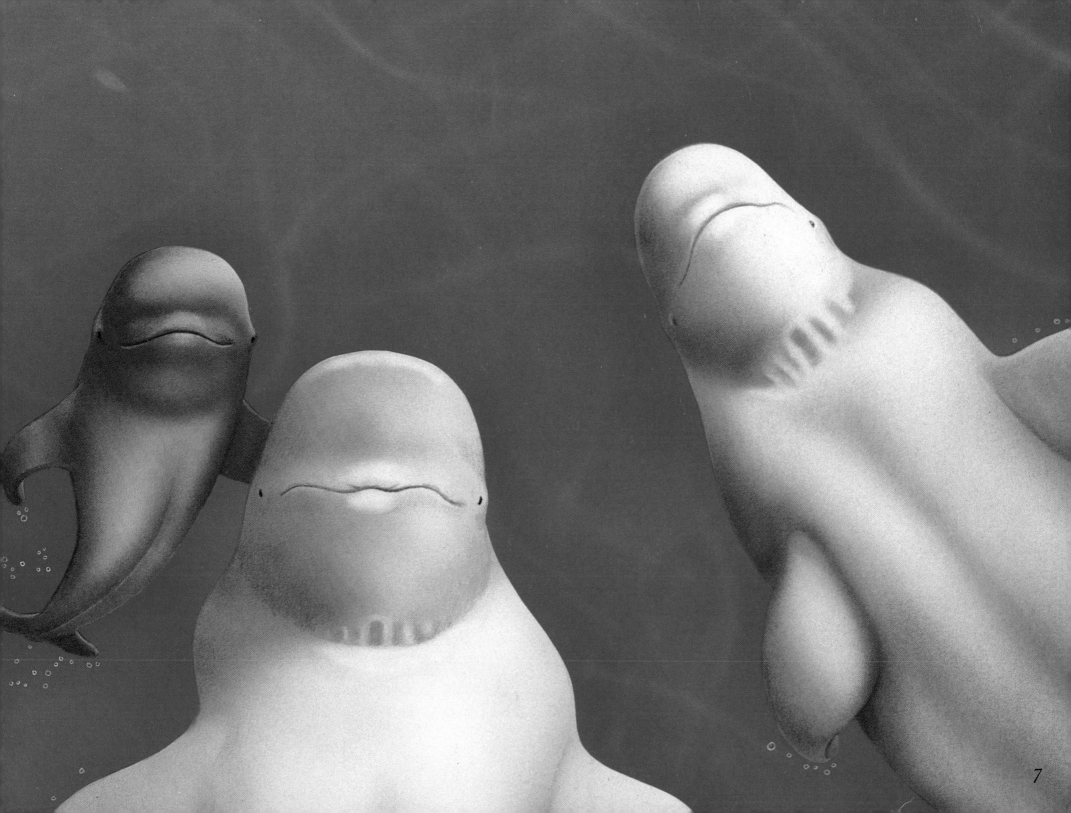

Hungry, Mother stops singing and dives deeper. Her head darts back and forth as she scoots along the ocean floor in search of food. She shoots jets of water from her mouth to uncover crabs and puckers her lips to suck up flounder.

Beluga Calf follows and tries to hunt, but she ends up with a mouthful of sand! She is only practicing — for months to come, she will live on Mother's milk.

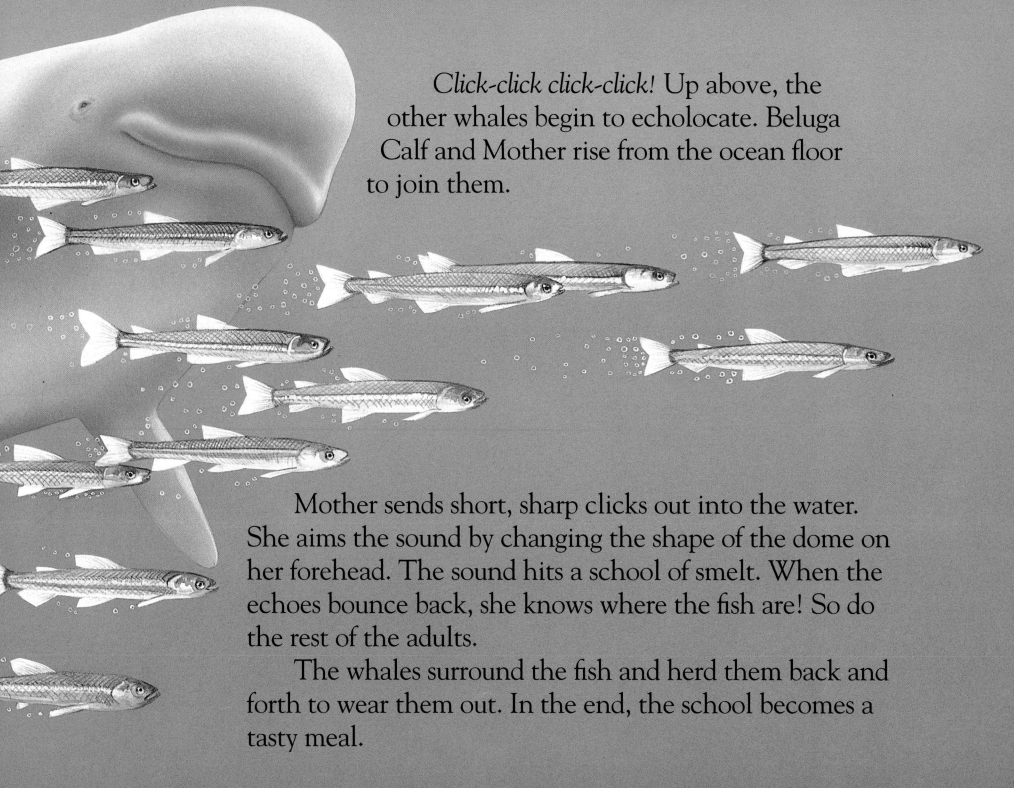

Click-click click-click! Up above, the other whales begin to echolocate. Beluga Calf and Mother rise from the ocean floor to join them.

Mother sends short, sharp clicks out into the water. She aims the sound by changing the shape of the dome on her forehead. The sound hits a school of smelt. When the echoes bounce back, she knows where the fish are! So do the rest of the adults.

The whales surround the fish and herd them back and forth to wear them out. In the end, the school becomes a tasty meal.

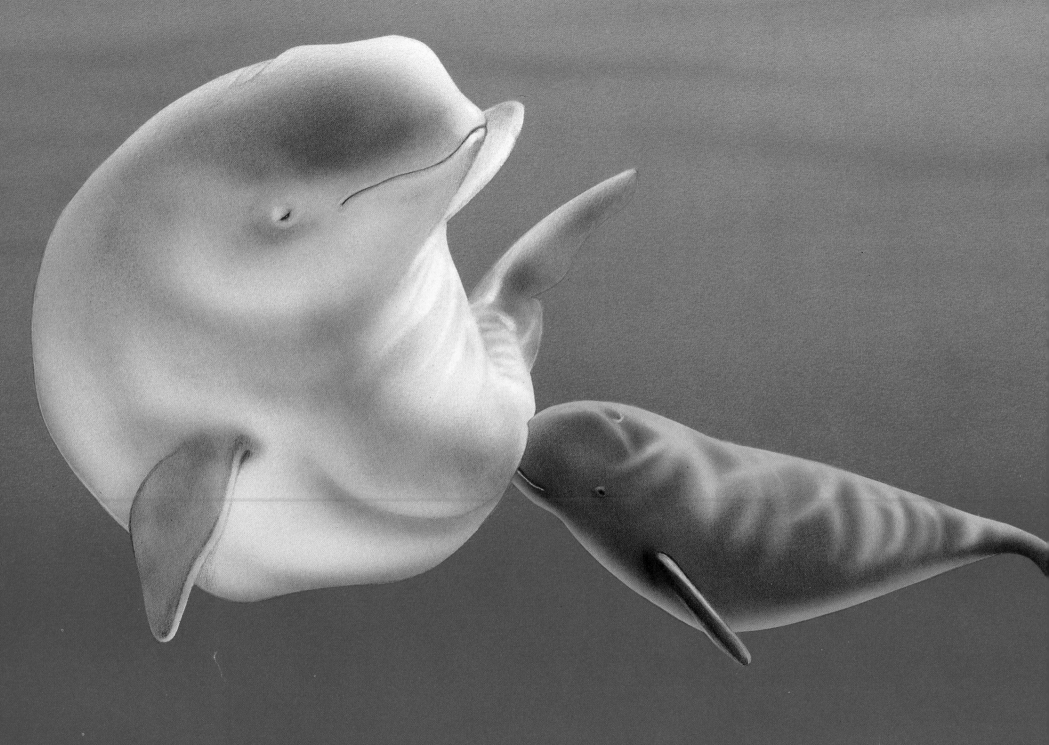

But the pod has fed too long. Already, the ice crust is creeping closer. The whales must move on. As they continue their journey, Beluga Calf and her friend swim close to their mothers, stopping only to nurse.

A while later, Beluga Calf is coasting in Mother's wake when the pod comes to a sudden stop. The belugas hear frightening sounds in the distance.

The noise grows closer and louder until the water trembles with clicks and screams. Black and white orcas burst into view. They are herding a pod of terrified narwhal, just as the belugas herded smelt.

The belugas scatter, trying to get out of the way. But Beluga Calf's friend is too slow. *Smack!* An orca slams into him as it charges after the narwhals.

As suddenly as they appeared, the giant hunters are gone.

The calf floats motionless in the water. Beluga Calf nudges him and whistles weakly to the pod. A chorus of replies brings the scattered whales back together.

The whales stroke the stunned calf with their flippers and gently lift him to the surface. Still he does not move. Beluga Calf circles nervously as the adults try again. This time, the calf breathes.

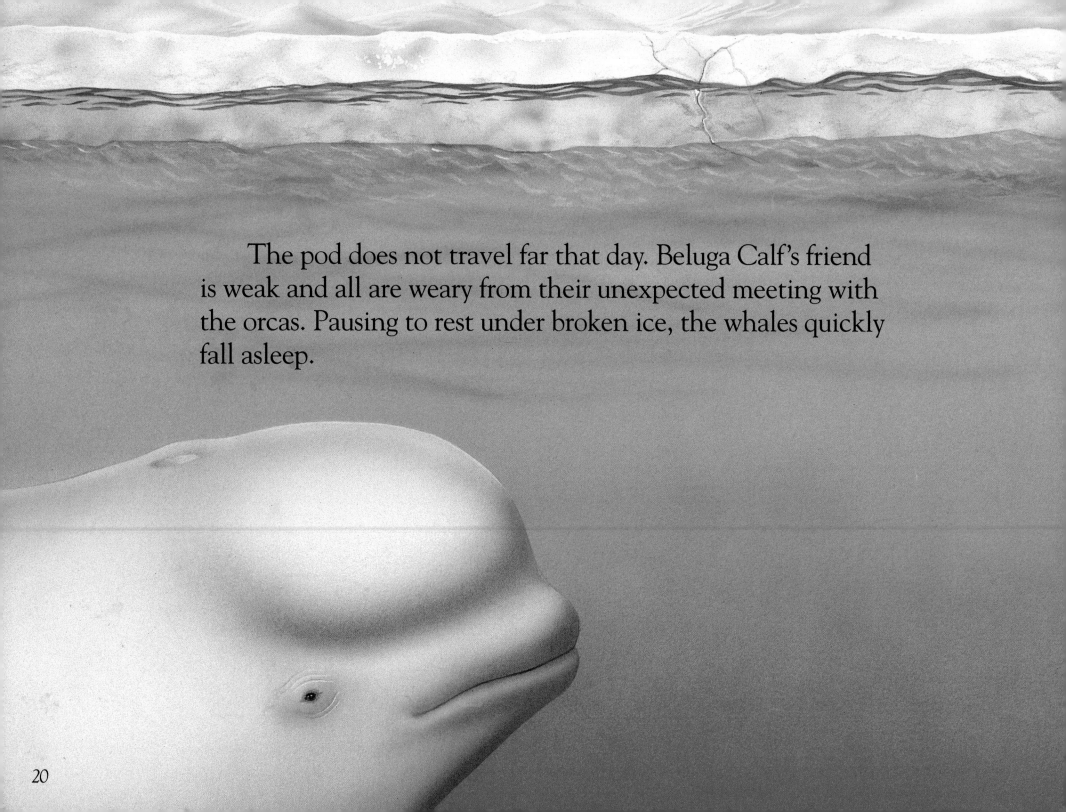

The pod does not travel far that day. Beluga Calf's friend is weak and all are weary from their unexpected meeting with the orcas. Pausing to rest under broken ice, the whales quickly fall asleep.

Hours later, Beluga Calf wakes up bumping against a hard surface. The ice has closed in to form a solid ceiling. How will she breathe? She turns to Mother for help. Beluga Mother knows what to do. Clicks echo through the water as she and the other adults seek out thin spots in the ice.

Swift and forceful,
Mother rams the ice with
the bumpy ridge on her back.
Crunch! Creak! The ceiling cracks.
Beluga Calf and her mother rush to the
opening and take in life-saving air. Steam rises from
their blowholes and freezes to form ice cones on their heads!

The whales do not linger — frosty
air and freezing water are warning signs.
They hurry south, rising to breathe
in breaks in the ice created
by other whales.

23

One morning, as Beluga Calf surfaces, she is startled to hear a beluga screeching. Beluga Calf looks across the ice at a strange creature. Though white, it is not smooth and slender like a beluga. It is coarse and heavy, and it does not sing. It snarls and growls.

With powerful teeth and huge paws, a polar bear has yanked a yearling beluga up through a hole in the ice. The wild-eyed whale thrashes about in a fight for his life.

Beluga Calf sinks beneath the ice, numb with fear. She sees
the yearling finally wrench free of claws that leave red stripes.
The yearling's pod has been circling anxiously nearby. Now
they warble and rub against him. His wounds will heal.

Splash! Splash! The polar bear's paws stir up the water again. The belugas watch silently. After a moment, the paws disappear. A bristly muzzle dips in and out. Polar bear feet thud overhead.

The belugas listen as the footsteps grow faint. The danger has passed.

Sensing that the journey's
end is near, Beluga Calf's
pod pushes forward. Finally,
the whales cross the Bering
Strait and leave polar bears behind.
They leap through the swells of the Bering
Sea joining other pods that have already arrived. Here
the ice is powerless, it only floats in broken chunks.

Beluga Calf and Mother race to the surface, then swoop back
down. They add their voices to a chorus of trills and whistles. All
around them white whales sing. The sea canaries have reached their
winter home.

About the Beluga Whale

Beluga whales are actually a kind of dolphin, or small-toothed whale. They are known by many different names, including "white whale" and "sea canary." Unlike most other dolphins, they often swim upside down and have flexible necks to let them turn their heads from side to side. Also, belugas lack the dorsal fins that many other dolphins have.

The name "beluga" comes from the Russian word "belukha," which means "white one." Beluga calves are born brown, dark gray, or blue, and become lighter gray at about one year of age, when they are called "yearlings." They don't obtain their white coats until they are full-grown. A full-grown male beluga can be as long as 18 feet, and weigh up to 3,000 pounds. The life span of a beluga is usually 25 to 30 years.

Glossary

blowhole: the paired nostrils on the top of a whale's head.

echolocate: to locate an object in the water through a series of high energy clicking sounds emitted from a beluga's blowhole. These sounds bounce off an object and echo back to the beluga, revealing the object's size, shape, and location.

flounder: flat fishes with both eyes on one side of their head; often they lie camouflaged on the ocean floor.

herd: a large group of whales, made up of many pods.

narwhal: a small Arctic whale, known for the long tusk that protrudes from one or the other of the male's upper jaws.

orca: also called the killer whale, or ocean dolphin, orcas are fierce hunters and often attack seals and other whales.

pod: a small group of whales that lives and swims together.

school: a large group of fish of the same kind swimming together.

smelt: small, slender fish sought by beluga whales.

wake: waves made by an object moving through the water's surface.

yearling: an animal that is between one and two years old.

Points of Interest in this Book